Are You Cross?

Wingman

By C.P. McClennan

AF373448

2   Wingman

Fiction

The Savannah Trilogy
Just Prey – Book 1
Darwin's Sword – Book 2
The Orphan War – Book 3

Wingman
Are You Cross?

Skelly Manor
1 – Snowbound 2021
2 – As Always, YMMV
3 – Brooklyn Storm   4 – Thawing Out
5 – Eat Your Heart Out
6 – War of the Moose Rider

A Cold Saddle – Scenes of Calgary, Vol 1

Tales of Director Jake

The Chronicles of Fifi

The Story of Fanny (editor)

The Pornstar's Husband
1 - Black Sheep Rising

Non-Fiction

The Adventures of a Polyamorous, Introverted and Atheist Husband
I – In One Convenient Package

wing·man

- a pilot whose aircraft is positioned behind and outside the leading aircraft in a formation.
    • a man who helps or supports another man; a friend or close associate.

"Which is more arrogant?

To assume that we are the only intelligent life in the universe, or to claim that there is other intelligent life out there that is just waiting to find us?"

- Master Jibberish

Prince Stefan's Apartment,
Downtown New Jersey City

"Are you cross?"

Cross allowed a slight glare. "That was not funny the first time you used it, never mind the several hundred times since."

"Only hundreds?" Prince Stefan laughed and slapped his shoulder.

Cross winced. Cordial as the intent may have been, the Prince packed a mean wallop.

"Yes, I need new jokes, Cross. There is not much more certain than that. Perhaps I should order you to write them for me. Can you write comedy, Cross?"

Standing at attention, Cross held his mouth shut. The fear that Stefan might command him to write jokes was real. It was unlikely the order would ever come, but he could not afford to take that chance.

"It's still a good one, though." After one further chuckle, Stefan hung his helm on the gold wall hook.

The epic struggle to take off his armor had begun.

Cross blinked and bit down on the inside of his lip. This was never easy to watch.

The armor, of course, was fake. Well, the armor was real enough, but there was no purpose for wearing it.

At best, it was cosplay.

It was not as if there were battles for Stefan to fight while wearing it.

Troops had not worn metallic, shiny armor for the past few centuries meant this was more cosplay than helpful. That troops didn't even exist at all meant he couldn't even wear it for inspections.

At best, the armor was cosplay.

The real battle, however, was avoiding scratches as Stefan took it off.

"I need you to keep lookout tonight," the prince said in muffled grunts while tugging at straps and buckles. He looked up at Cross. "Lady Angelica will be visiting tonight before she is off to her wedding."

Steel that once encased Stefan's left shoulder fell with a hollow clang on the floor, causing both men to jump and pause.

Cross winced.

So much for no scratches.

"I see, sir." Despite saying he understood, Cross was only half listening. It took Cross a moment and a long breath to catch up to what Stefan had said.

"You will need to keep watch for us and escort her to her waiting carriage after we are finished."

"Are we certain there will be carriage this time, sir? I mean, the last time..." Cross trailed off with his head shaking. "Sneaking women out is not the easiest of operations, in the first place."

"It will be there, Cross." Stefan picked up his goblet and gulped. The wine flowed past his lips and trailed along his muscled neck to soak into his undergarments. Armored only from the waist down, he clasped his hands at his chest as he looked around. He appeared lost on what to do next.

This was a familiar sign. It meant that Stefan had given up trying to figure out the rest.

Cross wanted to laugh but restrained himself.

Another constant battle.

Reaching over, Cross gave one strap a firm pull, causing the remaining armor to fall with a series of lesser clangs than the shoulder piece had.

A visit to the blacksmith for repairs would be required in the morning.

Collecting all the metal off the floor, Cross moved towards the closet to stow it away. His movements sounded like a percussion session in the process. During this, he spoke no words, waiting for the prince to continue.

"Cross! Do not damage the armor!"

Too late, Cross thought, but bit back this initial response. "Nothing that cannot be fixed."

"Alright. Make sure it's polished. I'll want to see my face shining in it when I need it next."

Cross could not stop his eyes from rolling at that one.

Luckily, the Prince did not see. He had moved onto his next thought.

Loving his own voice, Stefan did not allow for even a momentary pause nor segue before returning to the pre-armor subject. "She'll be here within the hour. We need to have her out your entrance by the time the clock strikes eleven. I'll also be needing you to watch that very clock for me."

"That very clock. I will notify you at eight o'clock. Yes, sir." This time Cross succeeded in not rolling his eyes but suddenly felt them squinting. Before his mind could apply brakes, he asked, "Hold on. My entrance?"

Stefan grinned. He carried his wine goblet and stepped towards the large bathing tub.

Unlike the armor, his undergarments put up no fight as Stefan sent them towards the same destination; the ground. Albeit, the fabric hit the ground with much less fanfare and noise than the armor had.

Stefan's answer began with a shrug. "Apparently, her future husband has my apartment under surveillance. He doesn't trust me or some such hullabaloo." He stepped the first of his muscled legs into the tub.

"I wonder why? But I ask again, my entrance?"

With a slosh, Stefan sat in the tub. "You know, the back entrance."

"I don't use the back entrance. I come in with you."

"You know what I mean, Cross." Stefan lifted his bath brush and waved it at Cross in dismissal. "The one you're supposed to be using. You know, if you were actually a real servant or something." He sent suds across the wooden floor like a priest spreading holy water amongst a crowd. There was no crowd here, however. Only Cross to mop it up.

Cross made a mental note to get a mop later. A moment later, he tore up the mental note, realizing Stefan would not need him while in the bath. "I'm going to get a mop."

Stefan held the tub sides tightly for balance as he sat down. "Good idea."

Better to get it done before Stefan and his femme du jour slipped and killed themselves. That would be awkward to explain on many levels.

"Of course, you know what I mean," Stefan continued, not seeming to realize Cross had turned away. "You are unmatched in your life experience, my friend. How could you not know?"

Cross froze, considering these words before deciding just how insulting they were. He turned to look back at the sudsed up man in the tub. "Are you calling me old?"

"Well, not in so many words." The grin on Stefan's face showed that, though still talking, he was preoccupied playing with a toy boat bobbing in the suds.

Yes, the same man in the shiny armor still liked bath toys.

"Hold on. Her future husband? She's engaged?"

Without looking up from his toy, Stefan nodded.

"Do you know any single women?"

Stefan laughed. "What fun would they be?"

Cross turned back and walked towards the apartment entrance, remembering a plot twist requiring a mop that needed to be developed. "I'll be back in a moment." Trying not to run, he left before the Prince could say anything further.

In New Jersey City's heart, the building was one of the Prince's favorite bachelor pads. The most realistic teak woodgrains holo-technology could provide decorated the walls. The only way it would appear more realistic is if it were cut from real trees.

It was not cut from real trees.

New Jersey had no trees.

There was no greenery at all.

The hall's walls were made from soil, fabricated into polymer walls. The walls would last four or five hundred years behind the teak projections, assuming no one demolished the place.

One day, when Stefan could afford it, weeping tile technology would be installed on the floors, making the basic mop completely obsolete.

Why have a mop when the holo decorators can cover a stain up until the tiles can soak away the liquids?

Criminal investigators were lobbying hard to ban the technology, but it was only a matter of time.

After slothing his walk down the hall, Cross came to the closet.

Sure enough, a mop hung stoically behind the door.

"One day, you will be useless, my friend." Cross pulled the wood-like handle down and stared at it. "Welcome to the club."

Laughter erupted from one of the other rooms, pulling Cross's attention away.

He shrugged and closed the closet door. He returned to the apartment at the same slow, plodding pace. As had been his hope, he arrived back in the apartment to find bath time was over.

Potentially being asked to write the Prince new jokes was much worse, but being ordered to play with one of the other toy ships was not much fun. It always ended with mysterious bruises on Cross as Stefan lost another tub ship battle due to poor tactics.

In this case, however, Stefan stood and was already dressed. He smiled, admiring his physique in the full-wall mirror. The Prince's hands moved like a magician performing to adjust his red silk ascot.

The ascot obeyed, allowing for it to be tucked into the collar of his black shirt.

The shirt was tight enough to show off his large chest and arm muscles before it tapered to his tiny waist. This was fashion, just as he liked it. His waist appeared slim due to the size of his shoulders.

Stefan was proud of these shoulders. He had once demonstrated his powerful shoulders by lifting Cross over them, regardless of Cross's squealing protests.

Cross, standing at attention near the apartment entrance, rolled his eyes at the memory. Being Cross was not a little man; the lift was rather impressive, even if it was totally gratuitous.

Speaking of total gratuitousness, Stefan popped his pectoral muscles before whistling at himself. With a quick spin, he checked out how tight his butt looked. "Outta sight," he growled. "Looking good, my man."

Tonight the Prince would play gigolo.

Tight clothing, slick black hair in a ponytail, and eyes the blue of Nottingham's skies. What woman could resist?

"Your physique is awesome, sir," Cross complimented. "As always."

"It is, isn't it? My calves look particularly good in these pants."

With Stefan still focused on the mirror, Cross allowed his eyes to roll once more. "That was the first thing that caught my attention. Calves like that, you should play football." Cross cringed as the words escaped his lips before he could stop them.

Stefan snapped his head to Cross and squinted. "Why would you bring that up?"

"I apologize. I wasn't thinking."

Stefan's squint turned into a look of concern. After a silent moment, he shrugged. "No worries, my friend. It is important to remember these things."

Relief washed over Cross.

Stefan turned back to the mirror. He then spun around.

Squirrel moment, Cross thought. This was his nickname for the moments when Stefan's mind latched onto something else entirely different from the subject at hand, like a dog on seeing a squirrel.

"Where is my sword? Have you seen it?"

Cross smiled. "Yes, sir. I stowed it away. I thought tonight you would be using a different type of sword."

Stefan glared at Cross for a moment. As the joke took hold, the glare softened. "That's a good one. Though my outfit still feels it is missing something, and Emma just might suffice."

Turning, Cross took three steps to Stefan. "How about we go full-rogue, sir?"

"How do you mean?"

Cross pulled at Stefan's shirt, untucking it from his pants. "I hear this is all the rage once." Stepping back, he smirked.

The untucked shirt left Stefan looking like he was wearing a frilly miniskirt. It was horrible, and there was no way he would...

Stefan smiled. "Full rogue. I like that."

Cross chuckled inside at tricking Stefan into a poor fashion choice. Being Cross had left the sword home at the castle, he was also pleased how easily

Stefan was distracted. "And the mighty sword, Emma, may rest quietly tonight."

A doorknock interrupted them.

"Come!" yelled Stefan.

An unseen servant opened the door from the outside, allowing Lady Angelica to drift in.

Her skirt was wide enough that she could have hidden a unicycle beneath it. Her black cloak offered hints of red beneath it.

The current fashion trend in such a dress was that it would hide a woman's feet. It gave the appearance that she was more hovering or floating rather than walking. As if the dress wasn't poofy enough, they added a specialized cloak specifically made to wear over the top of it.

"What do you think?" Stefan asked, holding his arms wide to show off his newfound fashion. "We're calling it full rogue."

Cross was no Don Juan, but he was reasonably sure that was not the appropriate greeting when one meets a secret lover.

"Full rogue?" Lady Angelica glanced at Cross. Though the words never crossed her lips, her eyes said in a direct tone, *You let him dress like this?*

Cross smiled at her as he moved close to take her black hooded cloak, revealing the red fabrics of the dress beneath.

He slipped the cloak off her bare shoulders and made a poor attempt to fold it over his arm. He was uncertain what else to do with this much fabric, but apparently, this was not it. Cross turned away to hang the cloak in the closet and avoid further awkward questioning glances from Angelica.

"Cross!" Stefan beckoned.

"Yes, sir?" Cross opened the closet and found an empty hook.

"Make sure she was not followed," Stefan ordered Cross.

Cross turned back to meet Stefan's gaze. No other words were required—just a quick nod before he made his way out of the apartment.

He walked down the hall to the front of the building. Opening one of the stained-glass doors, he stepped out into the cold and onto the front balcony. From three floors above the street, his view did not reveal anything out of the ordinary. A few carriages passed at street level below, oblivious to his watchful eye.

The sun had begun her descent, adding burgundy shadows to her tapestry by dipping behind a few of the buildings to Cross's left. There were enough shadows that could have hidden any of those not wanting to be seen.

"Monty Python would be proud," Cross said.

"Monty, who?" a familiar female voice to his right asked.

Cross spun and immediately felt the onrushing blood that would bring a blush to his cheeks.

Margreet, one of the Prince's maids, stood with a cigarette dangling from her fingers. "Python? Did you say

Monty Python?" A scarf over her head allowed only a few red curls out into the light. Her white frock had been chosen by Prince Stefan, no doubt more for its allowance for ample visions of cleavage than usefulness.

Cross nodded and returned his gaze to the street before she caught him staring at her gorgeous cleavage. It would have been awkward enough for him to get caught gazing into her green eyes, but not the cleavage. "An Old Earth comedy troupe."

"Old Earth?" She shook her head. "Not many talk of that."

Cross nodded toward the sunset. "Holo technology is wondrous, but I bet that doesn't compare to the real thing.

"I thought you were service gen?"

He nodded. "My father was a historian. I saw all the pictures and heard all the stories. I know them so well that I may as well have been born there."

She turned to lean on the black railing. "Oh, now that makes sense."

Glancing sideways at him, she offered the cigarette. "You wanna drag?"

"No, thank you. Those things will kill you."

"One can only hope. It's likely better than here." Margreet chuckled and pulled the cigarette towards her mouth. "Why are you out here, anyway? You like looking at pollution or something? Shouldn't you be in there watching the Prince shag that witch?"

"Lady Angelica is not a witch. She's a daughter of the Duke of..."

"I know who her father is. She's not very nice to us."

"Stefan is worried that she was followed."

"Paranoid, bastard." Margreet puffed smoke from her nostrils. "There wasn't anything out of the ordinary that I saw when the witch arrived."

Cross opened his mouth to protest titles again but thought better. He turned and found out just how quickly he could get lost in those big green eyes. "I believe you."

Margreet held the gaze for a moment before she began to giggle. "You fuckin', oaf."

Cross shook his head and snapped his eyes away. "Sorry."

"Nothing but the usual Hobgoblins roaming in the shadows." She put a finger to her lips as something seemed to occur to her. She tapped her cigarette on the railing to clear some ash. "You know, there was a black carriage across the street. It was there for a long while after she had come inside."

"Most carriages are black. I thought you said nothing strange."

"It was actual black, though. That was a bit strange, now that I think of it." Margreet nodded and pointed to where she had seen it. "Most of them are just covered in shit that makes them look black. This one was clean, even."

"Angelica hasn't been here long, though." Cross followed her gaze and squinted. "Not there anymore?"

She squinted before agreeing, "No. But it was there just long enough for it to seem a little odd." More smoke puffed from her mouth. "And the driver wore all white. That was strange."

"All white?"

She nodded. "Yeah, really bizarre." She tossed the cigarette out to the street.

"Yes, back to work for us both." Cross turned and opened the door for her.

"Thanks." She took a step half through and then stopped. She turned to look at him from the corner of her eye. "You know where my bed is. When the witch is gone, don't be a stranger."

"Oh, I couldn't."

"And why not?"

Cross could feel the red heat illuminating his cheeks.

Margreet laughed and turned away.

He followed her down the hall until he made a right, towards the Prince's apartment. As he walked in, his cheeks still burned at full blush.

Somehow, Angelica and Stefan were still exchanging pleasantries.

"Nothing there, sir," Cross reported. "At least nothing obvious."

"What, nothing?" Stefan asked in an annoyed tone. "What are you talking about?"

Cross felt confusion push the blood from his cheeks. That the couple was not yet naked had him thinking Stefan was truly afraid of potentially being caught.

Stefan had often appeared to experience a thrill at the possibility of getting caught, but this was different.

"You asked him to make sure I wasn't followed," Angelica growled at him.

Stefan nodded and turned his smile to Angelica. "Right. Sorry." He gave Cross a half-grin of further apology. Returning his eyes to Angelica, he asked, "Someone has me a touch preoccupied. Now, where were we?"

Angelica put her arms around his neck and linked them at her wrists behind him. "We were not yet quite here, but I think we should fast forward just a little." She pulled him in for a long kiss.

A mere moment later, Cross found himself shuffling around the bed, carrying an armload of clothing and pushing more around with his feet. There was too much to bring it all. He attempted to be as quiet and quick as possible while not disturbing the two on the bed.

He found what he deemed to be a safe distance from the bed. Where he attempted to fold and pile in two stacks upon the ornate table beside the sofa. He hoped that he had the sets separated correctly, but this was not as simple as it sounded with modern clothing choices.

What ever happened to shorts? And wood?

The ornate table appeared to be pure gold. It wasn't, but with the money Stefan spent on having it made, it may as well have been.

Feeling the clothes were now safe, Cross sat on the sofa facing away from the bed and picked up a book from the side table.

"Oh, yes, right there!" Angelica squealed. "Don't stop!"

The title on the cover of the book read, "Don Quixote."

"Seriously?" Cross whispered to himself and flipped it open.

"That tickles," Stefan said in a near howl. "Don't do that."

"Dohn do wha?" came Angelica's muffled reply.

Cross rolled his eyes as he considered telling her not to talk with her mouth full. Though, he was confident that someone, somewhere, would find doing that a compliment.

"There," Stefan growled. "Much better, yes, do...no, NO! That tickles again."

Focusing his attention on the book, Cross found the name of the translator, Thomas Shelton, on the title page in larger letters than that of the author, Miguel de Cervantes.

Cross dug into his pocket in search of a computer pad. A quick search derived that Mr. Shelton was the first to translate the book to English.

Cross chuckled as he wondered if this were one of the first translations or, like the golden table, just an ornate facsimile.

The Swiss-German, Swiss-French, or whatever language the book was initially written in would not have been something he could read. However, Shelton's old English version was not much better.

The words were recognizable, but the language had changed enough that it may as well have been a foreign language.

A glance back at the couple on the bed gave him an entirely new image of what it meant to tilt at windmills.

Angelica was impaling herself on top of Stefan's tiny erection.

Was impaling the proper term here? Pricking herself, maybe?

The questions went away as fast as it had formed.

That he had chosen to work for a Prince whose ego over-compensated for his lack of endowment on an hourly schedule was something Cross was certain comedy writers would love when the time was right.

Assuming that time ever came.

The stories of Old Earth proved that time might not ever come.

At least Stefan paid well.

Cross's breath vanished as his mind went to what it would be like sharing Margreet's bed for a night. No matter how much he wanted to enjoy a night listening to her talk and laugh while he snuggled into that bosom, it was not something he could easily give himself into doing.

Technically, she was a colleague, after all. The horror stories of workplace romances were all around, and Cross did not want to be on that list.

Unlike most people in this world, including the two slithering on the bed, he was not one for casual encounters.

He closed the book and studied the cover further as though looking for some sort of clue.

30 Wingman

His mind returned to one of his father's stories about their arrival in New Jersey.

***

53 Years Earlier
Bridge of The Starship Scott

Marshall Cross glared over his glasses at Renata Flemming. "I know you flew us here, but you can't be serious."

"Why not?" Renata stared right back, not flinching from his gaze. "I flew us here. I get to name it."

"I know, but..."

Arms folded across her chest; she leaned back in her chair. "I'm from Newark, so it is New Newark. The King said I get to name it."

It was not much of a bridge. The old science fiction stories had suggested it should be more like the old boats with people moving about to perform their duties.

The Starship Scott, however, offered a bridge that was only slightly bigger than the driver's space on an old city transit bus.

Marshall bent forward so his head did not scrape the ceiling. "We only just declared we're staying this afternoon. Can't you give it some time to think of a name?"

Her glare began to overpower his.

"Why not just call it New New Jersey?"

Her face softened. "I like it."

His hands flew in front of him with palms out to her. "No, that was a joke. Only a joke. That name is even worse."

She moved a hand to stroke her chin as if there was a beard to pull on.

Every good pilot should have a beard; real or fantasy was irrelevant. It was one of the known facts of the universe.

If nothing else, space travel tended to fuck around with what humans thought to be facts or laws of physics.

"It is absurd, and New Newark sounds no better." Marshall sighed and leaned against the console, half-seated.

"Don't you mess with my controls."

"I'm not messing, Renata."

"How about New Jersey, then?"

He pushed his glasses up. "Better. It doesn't sound like you're stuttering."

"New Jersey, the Second."

He opened his mouth for a moment before sound came out. "It's still better than New Newark."

"And New New Jersey," she agreed with a smile.

"We didn't travel all these stars to call it something stupid."

Renata shot up to stand, bumping her chest against him like he was an umpire. "Stupid!?!"

***

Prince Stefan's Apartment, Downtown New Jersey City

Cross never met the pilot, Renata. From all the stories about her that his parents told him, he learned a lot from her, even still.

Considering the run in she had with his father, Cross believed that *Dear Old Dad* was lucky to have out-lived her.

Before Cross's birth and only three months after landing at their new home, she was killed. An oxygen leak at one of the colony construction sites killed her and four others.

At the time, the colonists were still living on the ship until the Biodome was complete. It was almost a year before it was ready for the colonists to move in.

The very Biodome that gave holographic daylight and weather now. The same one that, due to population growth, had been expanded three times since.

Cross saw his own birth as proof his parents, neither being on construction teams, had too much time on their hands during that time. After all, he was the first infant born in the Biodome.

His father later shared that the week before her death, Renata had drunkenly admitted it had always been her intention to call it New Jersey, the Second. The entire New Newark idea was a scam so that his father, the writer who was documenting this trip, would accept the real name without question.

The Second portion of the name did not last, however. Within the first week, everyone had shortened the new planet name to New Jersey.

Cross's father said Renata even gave up correcting people before too long.

"Stop tickling!" Stefan screamed.

Cross's thoughts snapped back into the moment.

"Sorry, my darling," Angelica responded breathily. "Is this better?"

"No, NO, NO!!!"

"Wait. Actually, that's very good."

"Yes, just like that. Keep going."

"No, NO, NO!!!"

The room darkened as sunlight gave up on its daily effort. Candlelight in the room accepted the responsibility with pride. The only reason it was even lit was for ambiance, but it made no difference.

Cross continued flipping through pages without reading. The flickering light did not make reading easy, to begin with. It did, however, offer shadows of Angelica and Stefan dancing on the wall in front of him. The action stole his gaze occasionally away from the book, much as he tried not to look.

Stefan was a good man, though. After all the years working for him so far, Cross had become very fond of the prince despite being a royal egotistical idiot.

On the pro side of things, by the current monarchical standards, Stefan was downright progressive. Womanizer that he was seen as, he actually showed respect for women, whether in bed or not. The man just loved sex.

Even the lovely Margreet had once commented on how working under any other royalty member would have meant she would have to be proper and give up the smokes.

Her cleavage appeared in Cross's mind's eye, and his entire body sighed.

"Not there, Stefan! We talked about this. Don't do that."

"I'm sorry, my love. It is so tempting."

Turning to see what the issue was, Cross watched as Stefan pulled a finger from Angelica's ear.

Cross considered rewarding the couple by watching longer but returned to the book he was not reading. He reached for the candle beside him to pull it closer for better light.

Inevitably, the candle showed its appreciation for the gesture, rewarding him by dripping wax on his hand.

"Fuck," Cross hissed.

"Thank you, Cross," Stefan howled with a laugh that suggested they were now in a post-coitus state. "I think we have that covered."

"He could join us," Angelica suggested. "You could share me with your man."

Feeling the blush return to his cheeks, Cross ignored them. His mind turned to why technology had not solved the problem of scalding wax. His eyes drifted to the clock ticking in the corner.

At least the couple on the bed was now quiet enough he could hear the ticking again.

His eyes widened on seeing it. *Where the fuck has the time gone.* He gathered himself before standing. "Prince Stefan, please forgive the interruption."

"What is it, Cross? A little busy, here."

He turned to them. "I'm afraid your time for this evening is at an end."

"Should he be giving us orders like that?" Angelica asked. Angelica was draped over the top of Stefan. Both of their bodies were belly-down on the bed and still heaving for breaths.

Stefan smiled and allowed a single chuckle. "It's okay. I told him to keep an eye on the clock for us. We'd be lost without him." Stefan flipped over and gave one last kiss to each of her breasts.

She rolled off and laid on her back.

Climbing up on his knees, he turned to push his cock into her mouth one last time. His thrusts were slow and deep until his semen escaped her lips and dripped along her cheek.

Cross walked towards them and picked up a hand-towel from the side table to hand to her.

She wiped her face with it.

Cross retrieved the pile of clothing he believed to be hers and brought it to her.

"Thank you, Cross," Stefan said.

Angelica looked stunned. "You thank your servants?"

Stefan looked at Cross. "Who said he was my servant?"

Angelica opened her mouth but closed it again, not allowing for words. In a moment, she was up and dressed, sharing one last embrace with the still naked prince.

"Be safe, my love. Cross will take care of you from here."

She smiled at him and used her teeth to nip his bristled chin one last time. "Until next time."

He nodded. "A bientot."

"Mmmmm, French. You never cease to amaze me, my lovely prince."

Angelica offered no other words as she followed Cross out of the apartment and through the halls. Her coach waited at the back of the building, as was the plan.

Only on seeing the carriage waiting for her did Cross realize how nervous he had been. His stomach immediately unclenched. He also felt his shoulder muscles loosen.

As they stepped out in the alleyway, she turned to him and smiled. "I'm told that you are not a servant. With this in mind, I must thank you."

His eyes widened. "You only thank me because I'm not a servant?"

She sighed and smiled. "There is something very odd about you, Mister Cross. I'm not sure what it is, but you are very different."

He offered a non-committal grin in response.

She kissed his cheek. "And next time, you will share me with Stefan, no?"

"We will see."

"Most men would jump at such a chance with no hesitation. Most would have been tearing their clothes off and halfway to the bed when I mentioned the idea earlier. But you, sir, you are different." She reached down to his crotch. "Oh, my. I will enjoy that. Stefan might be jealous."

Cheeks now burning, he took her hand and helped her up the steps of the carriage. After securing the door, he stepped forward and looked up to the driver. "Get her home safe, my friend."

The driver looked confused at being addressed directly. "Of course, sir."

Cross nodded. "Thank you." He stepped back from the carriage and returned to the doorway. He glanced down the alleyway, both ways.

To his left, behind the carriage, some distance was another coach. It was black to the point of being eerie, even in the shadows of the surrounding buildings. Odder yet, the driver appeared to be wearing white.

"I told ya," Margreet's voice whispered behind him.

He spun to see her standing with her head poked out the door. "That's the carriage I saw earlier." She pulled her head in and stood straight to look up at him.

With a crack of the driver's whip, Angelica's carriage pulled away. It headed north with the slow clip-clop of horse hooves on the hard dirt.

Cross turned back and watched Angelica's carriage until it vanished past the buildings. Turning around, he found the other carriage had not moved.

"What is it?"

Margreet giggled. "A carriage. I dunno. Just fucking weird."

He turned to her and nodded. "That, it is."

"And look at that."

He spun back around.

"Gone," she said. "Same as earlier. No hoof sounds. Not an engine, even."

Space and rustling leaves were the only things remaining where the black carriage had been waiting.

"Ghostly," Cross whispered. "Could be electric, though."

"You think it's a spirit?"

"No." Cross shook his head. "I am concerned that Stefan is in over his head."

"That won't be the first time," Margreet said with a laugh. "He probably enjoys it."

He turned back to her. "You know him very well."

"You certain that it's not here for her?"

"I'm not certain of anything."

She lifted on her tiptoes and kissed him full on the lips.

His mouth parted and accepted her tongue to play with his own for a brief moment.

She broke the connection and lowered. "But I want to know you, sir."

He took a long breath. "I can't."

"You're married, aren't you? I don't care about that."

He smiled. "I am, but that's not why I can't."

"Strange carriages and strange men," she said, followed by a laugh. "What else does this evening have in store for me?"

"My marriage is hardly traditional." He waved his hand to dismiss the thought and suddenly regretted it for fear she might think he was dismissing her. He took her hand and lifted it to his lips. "I would love an evening with you, but..."

"So come see me when Prince Tightpants is asleep, Mister Non-Traditional Married Man. I don't care what your situation is. I just wanna fuck, and I wanna fuck with you."

He grinned. He could feel his penis rising to erection at the image Margreet had given him. "I'm not sure he will sleep tonight."

She pulled back from him, slowly cloaking into shadows inside. "You'll come when you're ready. Your mind just isn't there yet, but you'll come." She backed away and vanished into the shadows inside.

He smiled at the darkness.

Margreet shrieked.

His eyes widened in alarm as he rushed forward to find her. "What is it?"

"Stubbed my fucking toe," she whimpered. A giggle in the darkness followed and sounds of her hobbling off.

Retracing his steps, Cross found Stefan near sleep on the bed.

"Is she gone?"

"Yes, sir," Cross answered and poured into his own goblet of what little red wine the couple had left in the bottle. "One of these times, your schemes are going to fail. I'm scared to think how many little Stefans are running around thinking they are actual royalty." He opened a new bottle and topped off his beverage.

"She's gone, Cross. No more sirs tonight. Just Steff. And, you're right. Hopefully, I'll not meet a little unexpected Stefan-in-waiting anytime soon." Taking the bottle from Cross, he tilted it back to take a slug straight from it. Putting the bottle on the side table, he leaned back on the stack of pillows behind him.

"Go to sleep, Steff."

"Yes, sir," Steff answered, followed by an almost immediate inebriated snore.

Cross took the bottle and refilled his goblet again.

Stefan stirred with a grunt. "I owe you, Cross," he said in a muffled slumber voice.

"Of course you do." Cross put out the remaining candles with my wet fingers. "And you'll never repay that debt."

Stefan twisted and pulled one pillow in for a snuggle. "Now, Zorn Cross."

"Yes, sir?"

"Go bed that lovely Margreet. I don't want to see you until dinner tomorrow."

Cross could only answer with a lot of blinking.

***

Cross's Bedroom

Cross stared at the screen.

He sat at a small wooden looking desk. A refilled goblet of wine sat beside the monitor on top of the desk.

"Steve?" Cross asked.

The word, *Steve*, typed at the top of the screen.

The screen replied, *I'm here.*

"And?"

A few seconds of cursor flashing followed as though the computer were thinking. *I've heard of sightings of black carriages, like the one you described. Very odd, but only people observing it with no further detail.*

Cross lifted his drink and sipped. "Any that have seen it multiple times?"

Until your strumpet, Margreet, no. Not that I'm aware of.

"She's not mine, never mind my strumpet. Or anyone else's for that matter."

Whatever you say.

"How many sightings of the carriage?"

Dozens. All across Jersey City and even out into the Nanticoke Hills.

"Get's around then."

It's a carriage, of course it does.

Cross rolled his eyes. "Ok, I'll log off then. Let me know if you hear anything further."

Will do.

The chat session flickered off.

Cross spun in his chair and stood up. He grabbed his goblet and moved it to the bedside table. He pulled back the covers and slipped into the bed.

The candle on the bedside table flickered, asking to be extinguished.

Cross eyed the flame. "Not yet, my friend." He took another sip of wine before lifting a book from the table.

The same book he had liberated from Prince Stefan's apartment, earlier, Don Quixote.

"Let's tilt at some windmills, shall we?"

The wind outside let out a banshee's wail as it swept past his bedroom window. It was followed by pelting of rain.

***

On the Street

The driver wore white. She did not seem to notice the rain. Pulling back on her reins, she brought the equine androids to a halt. In turn, the black carriage beneath her came to a silent stop.

Falling rain had covered the hoofbeats of their approach, so it was unlikely any were alerted to the carriage's presence.

The rain was more lashing in the wind, than truly falling. It came diagonally, almost sideways. It was the type of rainfall that would sting an uncovered cheek of one out in it.

The driver, however, did not react.

"Which are we looking at?" the voice growled through the driver's earpiece.

The driver glanced up with blue sunken eyes in her silver face. The mechanical iris of each eye focused on the first window. "That is the Prince." The focus moved to a second, smaller window. "That is his man."

"Good," the voice approved.

"We were observed by his man, Zorn Cross, earlier."

"No consequence. Not yet, anyway."

The carriage rocked slightly as the occupant moved.

"Orders, sir?" the driver asked.

No response followed for two minutes.

The driver remained completely motionless, not reacting to the rain nor wind as the weather intensity increased.

"Someone is observing us," the voice finally responded. "It's the lower-level window, second from the left."

The driver turned slowly and found the window in question. Sheets of rain obscured her view and the mechanical irises were unable to adjust. Her hand lifted to touch behind her right ear and adjust something. Inside her eyelids, black lenses dropped and covered her eyes. "I can only make out a shadow, sir.

Uncertain whom it is. I believe that room may be occupied by one of the Prince's security team."

"That makes sense," the voice sounded relieved.

Keeping her hand on the controls behind her ear, she attempted to clear her vision further.

The rain had other ideas, increasing its rhythm even more.

Another moment of silence on the earpiece followed before the voice instructed, "Get us out of sight."

"Aye." The driver returned her eyes forward and lowered the hand from her ear to grasp the leather reins again. "I'm leaving my ocular lenses down, as this will be difficult to navigate without them."

"Don't leave them down too long," instructed the voice. "Your mother would tell you your face will stay that way.

"You're not my mother." She slapped the reins silently.

The equine androids and carriage began moving forward.

Author C.P. McClennan

Chris lives, writes and enjoys free thought in the mystical land of Toronto...he knows where his towel is, but he can't dance.

Twitter – @CPMcClennan

Facebook – Author C.P. McClennan

Website – www.cpmcclennan.com